# WHEN THE CLOCK STRUCK 12

## AUGUST 15 1947

**E Shailaja Nair**

Published by
Renu Kaul Verma
Vitasta Publishing Pvt Ltd
2/15, Ansari Road, Daryaganj
New Delhi - 110 002
info@vitastapublishing.com

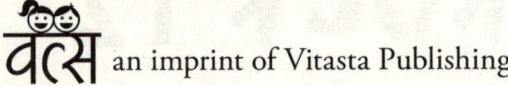 an imprint of Vitasta Publishing

ISBN 978-93-90961-24-5
© Vitasta Publishing
First Edition 2022
MRP ₹245

All Rights Reserved.
This novel is entirely a work of fiction. Names, characters, events and incidents are entirely imaginary. Reference to real places, actual regions, institutions or community practices has been made in a fictitious manner. Any resemblance to actual persons, living or dead or actual events is purely coincidental.

No part of this publication may be reproduced, stored in a retrieval system, or transmitted in any form, or by any means – electronic, mechanical, photocopying, recording or otherwise – without the prior permission of the publisher.

Layout by Balasundaram Kuppusamy
Printed by Vikas Computer and Printers

*For Praveen and Prashant, my first audience*

# CONTENTS

| | | |
|---|---|---|
| Acknowledgement | | vii |
| Prologue | | ix |
| 1 | A Queer Incident | 1 |
| 2 | Voices in the Night | 15 |
| 3 | To Chotu's Aid | 26 |
| 4 | A Mysterious Conversation | 39 |
| 5 | A Walk in the Night | 52 |
| 6 | The Plan | 61 |
| 7 | Sudden Discovery | 65 |
| 8 | Exciting Night | 74 |
| 9 | Chotu to the Rescue | 85 |
| 10 | Three cheers for freedom | 94 |
| Epilogue | | 99 |

# ACKNOWLEDGEMENT

This book came out of my attempt to teach my young son about Indian history, our freedom struggle, the sacrifices made by our leaders and why we should value our democracy, our freedom. To make history attractive for a 10-year-old, I would weave tales around historical events, just as my mother had done for me when I was a little girl. Thank you, Mom! Your bedtime stories made me into a storyteller.

I want to thank my Publisher, Renu Kaul Verma, who encouraged me to return to writing after a hiatus. I would also like to thank Alisha Verma, whose enthusiasm made the whole exercise fun and exciting.

Finally, I thank my young readers. You are the reason that I continue to write. I am sorry to say goodbye to Ashok, Priya, Asghar, Afshan, Chotu and all the other characters.

They have become my friends. I hope you love them as much as I do.

Shailaja Nair
5 July, 2021

# PROLOGUE

Praveen shoved his book into his desk and closed the lid with a bang as the bell rang for the end of school. Four full days of holidays! What glorious fun he would have.

"Hey, Praveen, aren't you ready yet? Hurry up, you slowcoach," said Prashant, heaving his schoolbag on to his shoulder.

"Coming. Let me just zip up my bag," Praveen said, suiting his action to his words. Picking up his bag, he followed Prashant to the school bus.

"Thank God, we haven't gotten too much homework," Prashant said as the bus sped towards their home. "I would have hated to sit and pore over my books when Priya Nani and the twins are here."

"Yeah, Payal and Amisha are coming here after such a long time. They came before they went to Canada to visit Asghar Uncle and Saeeda Auntie. And that is almost six months ago," Praveen said.

"Praveen, what are you folks doing these four days? My father is taking all of us to Jaipur," said Rohan, their classmate.

"We are staying in Delhi. Tomorrow being August 15 my grandfather says Delhi is the place to be in for Independence Day," Praveen explained.

"And anyway our great-aunt and cousins are coming over and they will be here for a week. They will go back only after Rakhi on August 18," Prashant said.

"Don't you feel thrilled when your cousins come over? You and Prashant are twins and so are your cousins," said Mala. "I wish I had a twin. How old are your cousins?"

"They are only six months younger than us. You won't believe this, but our grandfather's friend Asghar Uncle's grandsons, Iqbal and Javed, are also twins and so are his sister, Afshan Auntie's daughters Farida and Farah. And, what is more, they are also our age," Praveen said.

"Well, Asghar Uncle, Nanaji, Priya Nani and Afshan Aunty have been friends since they were children," Prashant said.

Before anything else could be said, the bus stopped and Praveen and Prashant hopped off. Waving to their friends, they set off for home.

"Praveen Bhaiya! Prashant Bhaiya! How long you've been. We've been waiting for you for hours," screamed

Amisha, running down the driveway. She was followed by Payal who had been lounging on one of the garden chairs on the verandah.

"How you exaggerate, Amisha. Your train must have come in about noon. And it is just about two now," said Prashant, giving her a hug. The four of them went into the house chattering nineteen to the dozen.

"Come in and look at all that we have brought for you," said Payal, dragging the boys to the guestroom. "We have brought tons of things from Iqbal, Javed, Farida and Farah as well."

Priya, the boys' great-aunt, and Payal and Amisha's grandmother, was busy unpacking the suitcases. Hearing the commotion made by the children, she turned round from the cupboard where she was hanging the twins' frocks.

"Namaste, Priya Nani," Praveen and Prashant said in chorus. "How are you?"

"I am fine. How are both of you?" she replied with a smile. "Payal, Amisha, you can hand over all the gifts. They are in that suitcase under the bed."

"But not till after lunch," said Praveen and Prashant's mother as she walked into the room. "Otherwise nobody will have any lunch before 4 o'clock."

Lunch was a special meal as all the children's favourite food had been prepared. There were aloo (potato) paranthas with thick curd and gulab jamuns to follow.

"Aloo paranthas remind me of my childhood," said Priya Nani, helping herself liberally to the curd.

"Does Asghar Chacha still love aloo paranthas?" the boys' mother asked, serving hot paranthas to the children.

"Yes, Mamiji, he adores them," said Payal.

"In fact, he said aloo paranthas remind him of the time that Nani and Ashok Nana helped save his family from danger," Amisha said.

"What danger, Priya Nani?" asked Prashant, blowing on his parantha to cool it down.

Priya Nani's eyes took on a dreamy expression.

"Those were troubled days, just after India had become independent. Ashok Bhaiya and I used to stay in this house while Asghar and Afshan's house was in the lane behind, where there is that big department store now. It was a lovely evening in August…"

# CHAPTER 1

# A QUEER INCIDENT

Ashok put away his books and looked longingly out of the window. It was such a lovely August evening, just right for play, and he had to remain cooped up. Mummy had left strict instructions that he should not leave the house. People feared there would be trouble in their locality too. Ashok sighed regretfully and picked up a storybook.

Though the book, which was about a boy who saved a whole town from bandits through his bravery, was open before him, Ashok's eyes were not on it. He looked wistfully at the playground, which was usually a hive of activity at this time of the day, but was eerily silent today. He got up and walked to the table that stood against the window.

If his friend, Asghar, had been here they could have worked on the "telephone". Ashok grinned to himself as he looked at what he and Asghar so ambitiously called the telephone. At first sight, it looked like a jumble of tin cans and wires.

Asghar and he had spent the whole of last week rigging a kind of telephone system between their homes using tin cans, wires, switches and bells. But so far it had not worked to their satisfaction. The day before, they had tried major modifications, but they had not had time to test it as yet.

As he stood contemplating the array of cans and other paraphernalia, a loud ring startled him. The bell on the table was ringing!

For a minute he was so surprised he did nothing. Then he picked up the tin can, which functioned as both receiver and transmitter, and said: "Hello! Hello! Asghar?"

He then fiddled with the switch, which was supposed to change the system to the transmission mode and held the can close to his ear.

"Hello! Ashok? Hey! Our telephone works!" Asghar's voice quivered with excitement.

Ashok could not keep the thrill out of his voice either.

"I still can't believe it," he shouted into the can. "Asghar, we have done it. Our telephone is a success."

It took them a few minutes to calm down.

"We have to still work on it," said Ashok. "Though I can hear you, it is not very clear. The volume too keeps fluctuating. But I don't know when we will be able to get together and work on it again."

"Ashok, what are you doing?" Asghar asked. "I am bored stiff, but Ammi said I was not to go out today. Such a pain, isn't it?"

"Oh, it is," Ashok agreed, vehemently.

Asghar let out a loud sigh and said: "Anyway the fact remains that we can't go out to play today. I had hoped to continue the cricket match we began yesterday. I am dying to defeat your team in revenge for the drubbing we received yesterday."

"As if you would be able to," Ashok retorted. "We are too good for you. You don't have bowlers and batsmen as good as ours."

"You are lucky that you are so far away or I would have punched your nose for a remark like that," Asghar said.

Ashok merely laughed. "Listen Asghar, I think Ma has just returned. I heard her going upstairs. I'll talk to you later. Bye!"

Replacing the can on the table, Ashok ran out of the room and upstairs to Ma's room.

Ma was taking off her sandals and changing into chappals.

"Ma, what happened at your meeting?" Ashok asked. "Are the rumours true? Is it a fact that people are being killed and that policemen are patrolling the area? What are you going to do about it?"

"Enough, enough, Ashok," Ma protested, laughing though her eyes were sombre. "What a walking question mark you are!"

"Come on, Ma, I want to know what is happening in the city. Obviously you were worried or you wouldn't have forbidden us from going out," Ashok said in an impatient tone. "Is it true that Hindus and Muslims are killing each other?"

Ma's face lost all traces of laughter.

"Yes, it is true," she said. "But they are being instigated by a few people who are actually friends to neither the Muslims nor the Hindus. For a true Hindu or a true Muslim will never kill or tell others to do so."

Ma looked at the clock on the dressing table. It was almost seven in the evening.

"Well, let us go downstairs," she said. "It is getting late and soon Papa will be asking for dinner. I hope Asha has finished cooking."

Just as Ma and Ashok turned to leave the room, Ashok's

younger sister, Priya, came in. She had a puzzled look on her face. Seeing her mother, she ran to give her a hug.

"I didn't know you were back, Ma," she said. "I was looking for Bhaiya."

"Why were you looking for me, Priya?" Ashok asked. Before she could reply, Ma, noticing the look on Priya's face, ruffled her thick black hair and said, "What is worrying my little *gudiya*?"

For a minute, Priya's round little face lost its worried look as she smiled at her mother.

Then she said, "Ma, I was standing by the window of the drawing room when I saw two men at the end of our lane. Soon, a couple more men joined them and they began talking together. They seemed quite angry and one of them pointed to a house in the lane behind ours. Another man immediately pulled down his hand. Then a policeman entered the lane from the other end and the men quickly walked away."

As Priya narrated her tale, Ma looked more and more worried. When Priya stopped, Ma patted her shoulder and said, "Don't worry Priya, I will talk it over with your father."

"These are really troubled times," Ma mumbled to herself as she went downstairs. She was deep in thought.

"I wonder what will happen now that India is free. All these days we thought that freedom from the British would solve all our problems. But it seems only to have created new ones. It is like a madness. Muslims are killing Hindus and Hindus are killing Muslims. It is all so senseless."

She remembered what she had read in the newspaper that morning. Gandhiji had appealed to everyone to stop the killings.

It seemed difficult to believe that only a week ago everyone had been so happily celebrating India's independence at the Red Fort. What a party there had been on the streets! Everyone was out till the early hours of the morning. All faces wore big smiles and there had been none of this enmity that was rocking the country now.

The memory of Pandit Jawaharlal Nehru's speech in the Council Hall of Parliament House still made her nerves tingle and her blood run faster. Ma went over the words in her head.

"Long years ago, we made a tryst with destiny, and now the time comes when we shall redeem our pledge, not wholly or in full measure, but very substantially. At the stroke of the midnight hour, when the world sleeps, India will awake to life and freedom.

"A moment comes, which comes but rarely in history, when we step out from the old to the new, when an age ends, and when the soul of a nation, long suppressed, finds utterance. It is fitting that at this solemn moment we take the pledge of dedication to the service of India and her people and to the still larger cause of humanity."

But all that jubilation and ecstasy had given way to sorrow and death. Now there was such a pall of gloom everywhere. Ma shook her head in sadness as she walked into the kitchen.

"Bhaiya, Ma is looking quite troubled," Priya said after Ma left the room. Ashok too looked worried.

"I think your news about those people is bothering her," he replied.

"But why, Bhaiya? Of course, they didn't look very nice people, but why should Ma be so worried?"

"You know the sort of rumours we have been hearing. And there are a few Muslim families living nearby. What if those people were planning to harm them?" Ashok said.

"Bhaiya, I suddenly remembered. Asghar and Afshan live in the lane behind ours. Heavens, I hope those people were not planning on doing anything to Asif Chacha and Nafisa Chachi," Priya said.

Ashok went pale. For a minute, he had forgotten that his best friend was a Muslim and that he lived in the lane behind.

"Bhaiya, we must do something to warn them. Afshan is not even well. You know she has been down with fever for more than a week." Eight-year-old Priya was almost in tears. Asghar's sister Afshan was her best friend and she couldn't imagine anything happening to her or her family.

"But what can we do?" Ashok asked.

Just then they heard a knock on the front door. They ran downstairs. As they reached the bottom stair, their father came out of his study. He motioned the children to be quiet and went to the front door. He peeped through a crack between the slats.

"It is Srivastava," Papa said in a relieved voice. He drew back the wooden bolts and opened the door to welcome one of his oldest friends.

Ashok and Priya too ran to welcome him. Srivastava Chacha was a favourite with them. He shook hands with Papa, thumped Ashok on the back and swung Priya high above his head. Priya squealed in delight.

"Hello, everybody!" he greeted. "I hope you will ask me to stay to dinner, Bhabhiji. I am so hungry, I could eat a horse."

"Of course, Bhaisaab. You know you are always welcome," Ma said, drawing her dupatta across her shoulder. She bustled away to put the finishing touches to dinner.

Dinner was a hilarious meal thanks to Srivastava Chacha. He kept them in perpetual laughter with his jokes. He had a knack of saying the silliest and funniest things with a perfectly straight face. He pulled Priya's leg mercilessly.

"Srivastava Chacha, the last time you met us you said you were due for an operation. Did you have it?" Priya asked.

"Of course, I did," Srivastava Chacha replied.

"Was it very painful?" Priya was very sympathetic. She herself could not stand even the prick of an injection needle.

"Not at all," Srivastava Chacha replied. Priya was puzzled. How could anyone say that an operation was not painful? Suddenly her face brightened. "Oh, you mean you were under anaesthesia," she said.

"No way. I was fully conscious throughout the operation," Srivastava Chacha said proudly. Priya was suitably impressed. He was really brave, she decided.

By now Papa, Ma and Ashok were sure that Srivastava Chacha was pulling Priya's leg. They started to giggle. Priya looked at her family in surprise. What was wrong with them? She turned back to Srivastava Chacha.

"Chachaji, what was the operation you underwent?" she asked.

"Well, it was quite a serious one. I had my hair cut!"

This finished off the rest of them and they dissolved into helpless laughter. Priya was most indignant at being made a fool of in this manner. She jumped off her chair and ran to Srivastava Chacha and began pummeling him.

"That is enough, Priya," Ma said. "Go back to your

chair and finish your dinner." Priya returned to her place and the meal continued in peace.

After dinner, Srivastava Chacha and Papa retired to the *baithak* (seating area), while Ma went into the kitchen to give the maid instructions about next day's breakfast. Ashok and Priya went to their room.

The children's room was large, roomy and tastefully furnished. It was in one corner of the house so that even if they were playing noisy games they did not disturb the grown-ups.

There were two large windows: one facing the east and the other west. As a result, it was bright and sunny throughout the year. The east-facing window overlooked the road, just as the windows of the drawing room did further down the corridor, while the west-facing one opened into the garden.

A broad window-seat was built at the garden-facing window on which were flung gaily coloured embroidered cushions while a table stood against the other one. There was a huge couch in one corner and one wall was covered with cupboards, which held the children's books, toys and other knick-knacks. Two chairs were pushed against the study table, which stood in the middle of the room.

Ashok and Priya loved their room and spent practically all their waking hours there, only going upstairs to their bedrooms to sleep.

Now they came in and settled down with a book each. Priya curled up on the window-seat and was soon lost in a world of fairy tales while Ashok picked up one about the adventures of King Vikram and Betaal. Usually the children loved reading, but today they found it difficult to concentrate on their books.

After about 15 minutes, Priya looked up from her book and said, "Bhaiya, do you really think there is any danger to Afshan's family?"

"I can't say anything for sure, Priya," Ashok replied. "But you know that the last few days have been bad. We have heard rumours of many people being killed. And I know that Ma is worried."

"Can't you think of any way of helping them?" Priya asked.

She looked hopefully at her brother. Eleven-year-old Ashok, tall for his age and thin, seemed quite grown up to her, someone able to solve most problems and difficulties.

"But what can we do?" Ashok asked in return. "We don't know what the men are planning. And even if we knew for sure that they were going to harm Asghar's family, there is no way we can inform him about it. Mummy has said that we are not to leave the house till the situation in the city improves."

"But we can't just sit here and do nothing, Bhaiya," Priya said in a shocked voice. Ashok did not reply. He wanted to help Asghar, but could not imagine how this could be done. Priya's eyes went to the cans and wires spread out on the table.

"Can't you use that, Bhaiya?" she asked pointing to the "telephone".

"You know we haven't finished with it as yet. But now that you remind me, Asghar did manage to get through today. Maybe I can call him up," Ashok said, getting up and walking towards the table.

Ashok began to fiddle with the wires. Then he picked up the transmitter-cum-receiver and held it to his ear. His eyes lit up as he heard the faint tinkle of the bell. But alas! He heard a crackle and a snap and then there was total silence. He fiddled with the wires trying to get it to work again, but in vain.

Just then they heard Ma calling them, asking them to get ready for bed. They began putting away their toys and books. As they shut the cupboard, Ma came in.

"Come on now, hurry up, children," she said. "Have your bath and go to sleep."

"But I am not sleepy, Ma," Priya protested.

"It is past 9.30 and you are later than usual," Ma said.

"But I am really not tired or sleepy," said Priya again.

"You can read for fifteen minutes after you are in bed if you promise not to lie down and read," said Ma, giving in to Priya's pleas. As they were leaving the room Ma added: "But if I find you wandering around the house after you are supposed to be in bed, Ashok, I will make you go to bed an hour earlier tomorrow."

Ashok went red. One night, the week before, when he could not sleep, he had wandered down the corridor to the window at the end and stood looking out. Ma had caught him standing there and had been very angry. Wishing Ma goodnight, Ashok quickly walked out of the room. Priya followed on his heels.

"Well, what do you think of Priya's tale, Srivastava?" asked Mr Gupta, the children's father, a little while later. They were in the baithak discussing what Mrs Gupta had told her husband earlier in the evening.

Mr Srivastava looked serious. "I do not know what to make of it," he said. "Considering the situation in Delhi and the fact that there are some Muslim families in our locality, I think we should alert the committee."

"I agree with you. I think it was a really good idea to form a neighbourhood security committee. If we, the neighbours, remain united nobody can harm us."

"Well, Gupta, I think I will take my leave now. It is getting late and my wife will be getting worried."

"OK. We will meet tomorrow as planned. And you can drop in at Arora's house on the way and tell him to alert the committee."

"I will do so. Say goodnight to Bhabhiji for me," Mr Srivastava said.

Mr Gupta closed the door after Mr Srivastava left and made sure that all the bolts were secure. Then he went upstairs, a thoughtful look on his face.

## CHAPTER 2
# VOICES IN THE NIGHT

Ashok and Priya ran up the stairs.

"Race you to the bathroom," Priya shouted. Forgetting about his friend's possible troubles for a minute, Ashok too raced up the stairs, taking them two at a time. He just beat Priya to the bathroom and she was left banging at the door in frustration.

"Stop that noise, Priya," Ma called from downstairs. Priya left off the banging and went to the bedroom to wait for Ashok to come out.

Ashok and Priya shared a bedroom, which was at one

end of the landing. It was like two rooms without a door in between. This gave both of them some privacy, but they could also talk to each other while in bed. Priya, who had a dreamy nature and loved the moonlight to fall on her face, had her bed close to the wide window.

Ashok's bed was in a funny little alcove sort of place, standing against another window. Bright multi-coloured rugs were strewn across the floor. In one corner was a huge cupboard that they both shared. Opposite the cupboard was a dressing table, chockful with Priya's dolls.

As Priya waited, she folded back the brightly embroidered bedspread and opened the curtains. Soon Ashok walked in, still rubbing his wet hair. He was grinning at having got the better of his sister.

"Your turn, slow coach," he said. Priya picked up her nightdress and making a face at him, ran out of the room.

When she returned to the bedroom, Ashok was just getting into bed. Priya grinned to herself as she saw him trying to push his legs under the coverlet. He was going to get a shock. A look of surprise appeared on Ashok's face. He could not push his legs down. He pushed harder and squealed as he felt something prick his feet.

It was then that he noticed Priya rolling in her bed with laughter. Realisation dawned on him. She had made an apple pie bed for him in revenge for having beaten her to the bathroom. He gingerly disentangled the coverlet and the sheet and picked up the hairbrush (this was what had pricked his feet) which Priya had added for good measure, and flung it at his sister. But Priya ducked and the hairbrush bit the cupboard with a loud noise.

"Ashok! Priya! If you don't stop that noise immediately and get into bed I am going to be very angry," Ma called out. They stopped fooling around and got into bed.

Priya leaned against the pillows and opened her book. It was then that Ashok remembered that he had left his book downstairs.

"Oh, no!" he exclaimed, startling Priya into dropping her book.

"What is wrong now?" Priya asked, bending to pick up her book from the floor.

"I have left my book downstairs," he said. "I'll just run down and get it."

"But suppose Ma catches you? She will be furious," Priya said.

"I will be careful. I will return in a jiffy," Ashok said.

"Bhaiya, do hurry," replied Priya, going back to her book.

Ashok tiptoed to the door and peeped out. There was nobody on the landing. He crept out of the room and went to the head of the stairs. He could hear voices downstairs—Ma talking to Asha, the maid who was washing the vessels; Chotu, the little boy who did odd jobs around the house, scolding the cat for sleeping on his mat; Papa and Srivastava Chacha conversing in the baithak.

He decided that it was safe to venture downstairs. Keeping to the side of the stairs closest to the wall, he silently tiptoed down, testing each step before putting down the other foot. He was halfway down when he heard the tinkle of somebody's payal (anklets). He pressed himself against the wall and waited with bated breath. Was it Ma coming to see whether he and Priya were in bed? If it was, then he was in deep trouble. But it was only Asha going to the storeroom. Soon he heard her return to the kitchen.

Once the coast was clear, he ran down the remaining steps silently. As he reached the last stair, he heard Papa and Srivastava Chacha come out of the baithak. He quickly slipped into the little space underneath the stairs and hid.

He heard Srivastava Chacha leave. Papa closed the front door and went upstairs. Once Papa's footsteps died away, Ashok ran on tiptoes to the playroom.

The room was in darkness. He dared not switch on the light in case Ma saw it and came to inquire. Ma was lovely, but she hated disobedience of any kind. If she caught him here at this time of the night she would be most annoyed.

As his eyes got used to the dark, Ashok saw his book lying on the table near the window. He went to pick it up. He was about to turn and leave when he noticed that the window was not completely shut. Obviously Chotu had been in a hurry and had hastily closed the shutters.

Ashok stretched out his arm to shut the window properly. And he froze. Someone was whispering. At first he could not make out where the whisper came from. Was there someone inside the room? But who? And where? Then he realised that it was coming from outside. Someone was in the lane. In fact two or three someones. They were not talking to him, but among themselves. But who could be there at this time? He looked at the luminous dial of the clock on the table and found it was half-past eleven. Anyway it was not his business. He shrugged his shoulders and leaned across to reach the handle of the shutter.

Suddenly he heard someone mention Asif Khan. Immediately he became alert. Asif Khan? Were they talking of Asghar and Afshan's father? Silently, he moved closer to the window and pressed his ear to the crack.

"We will creep in at midnight while those Muslims are asleep," said one voice.

"Yes, that would be the best time. Nobody will think of keeping as strict a vigil now thanks to Mahatma Gandhi's assurance that no Muslim will be harmed in free India," said another voice.

"But have you warned Ramu to be ready to open the door for us?" asked a third voice.

"Oh yes. That was a good idea of yours, Vishnu, to ask Ramu to get into the house as a Muslim servant. We will not have any problem whatsoever. And as Ramu was brought up by Muslims after his parents' death, no one will suspect him. These Muslims should learn that if they want a country of their own, then they had jolly well go there and leave India for the Hindus," said the first voice.

"Yes, and at long last I will be able to take my revenge on Asif Khan for dismissing me from his factory," said the second voice in a savage tone.

Ashok heard the people move away after that. He stood there for a few more minutes. Once he was sure that there was no one outside he closed the shutters and went out of the room.

The house was in total darkness. Everyone had gone to bed.

"I wonder what the time is." Ashok asked himself. "It must be quite late." Just then he heard the huge grandfather clock in the dining room strike midnight.

"Gosh! I had better hurry up to my room. I did not realise I had spent so much time in the playroom. If Ma catches me now there will be the devil to pay." And he ran upstairs lightly.

The bedroom too was in darkness. Priya was obviously asleep. Ashok quickly got into bed.

But he could not sleep. His mind was in turmoil. He could hear Priya's even breathing. He debated whether to wake her up and tell her everything. But what was the use? She would only be upset. At present she was fathoms deep in a peaceful slumber. He let her sleep.

Ashok lay awake for a long time going over all that he had heard. Obviously Asghar and his family were in grave danger. But what exactly the danger was, he was not sure of.

"What will those horrible people do to Asghar and the others?" Ashok wondered. "Will they be killed? Or is it only a plan to rob them of their valuables?"

He didn't know when the dastardly deed was to be done either. The men had said midnight, but not the day. Was it tomorrow? Or the day after? Or the day after that?

Ashok tossed and turned restlessly. Maybe it was a plan to kill the Khans. After all they were Muslims and the men who had been talking in the lane sounded like Hindus. And these days, killings were going on all over the city.

With all the tossing and turning his bedclothes were in a thorough mess. He decided to get up and remake his bed. He had to be careful not to wake Priya.

Once he had made his bed he found he was still feeling wide-awake. He was thirsty too. There was a *surahi* (earthen pitcher) on a table outside in the corridor.

Ashok went out of the room, picking up a glass from the table on the way. He tilted the surahi and filled his glass with cool water. Picking up the glass he walked to the window at one end of the landing.

It looked out on to the garden at the back of the house. He opened the window and sniffed the fresh night air. Summer was over and there was the lovely smell of wet earth that he associated with the monsoons. He stood there for a while sipping the glass of water.

The garden was shrouded in darkness. The moon was behind a large cloud. Here and there he could make out some dark shapes of rose bushes, covered with blooms, which spread such sweet fragrance in the garden during the day. It was a haven for bees and butterflies when the sun shone.

The garden was a favourite resting-place for the whole family. Papa loved to sit under the huge pipal tree and read while Ma's favourite place was near the rose bushes. She would lay out a charpoy there and do her sewing on summer evenings and knitting on winter afternoons. Priya and he loved to spread a rug under the neem tree in the corner and play games or read. Usually they would be joined by Asghar and Afshan.

Thinking of his friend brought back to Ashok's mind all that had happened earlier. Again and again the same questions went round in his head. What should he do? How could he help his friend and his family? He heard the clock downstairs strike one.

"Well, no purpose will be served if I stand and worry just now," he told himself. "Maybe when I wake up in the morning, I might be able to think of some way out. At present, I had better go back to bed." And he returned to his room. As soon as his head touched the pillow, he fell asleep. He forgot that he had left the glass on the windowsill.

Meanwhile in another part of the city, people huddled together in their houses while a pitched battle raged outside.

It was a locality where most of the families were Muslims. The few Hindu families who had lived there for generations were now too scared to even leave their houses. The children were crying, scared by the loud noises, while the women sobbed under their breath, praying to God to keep them and their families safe.

Outside on the road, instigated by a few trouble-makers, people who had been friends since childhood were fighting for each other's blood. Anything they could lay their hands on, were used as missiles. Broken bottles, bricks, stones, lathis and knives were used freely.

Though being fought in the name of religion, the battle was the result of momentary senseless frenzy—for anyone who stopped to think realised that neither religion preached violence.

Soon the police arrived and after about an hour, an uneasy calm settled on the area. But everyone knew that the trouble was not over. It had only been suppressed by the stern hand of law and could burst out again any moment. It would not take much to restart the furious fighting.

Once the troublemakers had been removed from the area, the place looked a thorough mess. There was broken glass, bricks, stones and blood everywhere. A few wounded persons were still hanging around, moaning in pain. Gradually even they went off. What was once a peaceful and lovely park was now completely spoilt. Plants had been uprooted, fences smashed and flower beds trampled.

In the hospital nearby, despite the lateness of the hour there was hectic activity. The Casualty was buzzing. Doctors and nurses rushed from patient to patient trying to attend to the steady stream of wounded coming from the riot-hit locality. While some needed only first aid, some had to be admitted while yet others were beyond human help.

The next day's paper reported: Communal riots claim four lives.

## CHAPTER 3
# TO CHOTU'S AID

Ashok woke up the next morning to the sound of someone crying loudly. He lay in his bed for a minute trying to organise his thoughts. His midnight excursions had left his mind groggy. Suddenly the cries were heard again. Who could it be? It seemed to be coming from the yard below.

"That sounds like Chotu's voice. I wonder what is wrong with him," Ashok muttered to himself as he threw off the bedclothes and got up. He ran to the window. What he saw there made him exclaim loudly.

He came away from the window and quickly changed his pajamas for shorts. He was tucking in his shirt when Priya woke up. She sat up in bed and rubbed her eyes. The same cries had woken her up too.

"What is all that noise, Bhaiya?" she asked.

"The gardener, Kumar, is beating Chotu. I am going downstairs to find out why," Ashok said, running out of the room. He sped down the stairs, leaping the last three in his hurry to get to Chotu.

"Kumar, Kumar! Why are you beating him?" Ashok cried as he ran out of the house. He tried to stop Kumar from dealing out any more slaps. Chotu was crying piteously. His shirt was torn where Kumar had pulled it and his cheeks were swollen from the slaps.

"Don't stop me, Ashok Baba," Kumar said, his voice trembling with rage. "This thieving lad has stolen the silver lamp which was kept near the *tulsi* (basil) plant in the garden. To think that I took pity on him and brought him here from the village. I thought he could learn how to become a good servant and earn some money instead of starving to death there. Maji and Babuji have been so kind to him and this is how he repays them." Kumar lifted his hand to slap Chotu again.

"No, no, Ashok Bhaiya, I didn't steal the lamp," cried Chotu, cowering before Kumar's raised hand. "When

I locked up the doors and windows last night the diya was there near the tulsi plant. I saw it."

"Not only do you steal, you have learnt to tell lies too," Kumar thundered. "I will beat you to death if you don't tell me immediately where you have hidden the diya."

"I didn't steal it," sobbed Chotu. Kumar dealt him another stinging slap.

"Bhaiya, make him stop," cried Priya, who had joined Ashok in the yard. She pulled at Ashok's arm to make him listen. Ashok didn't know how to stop Kumar. Freeing himself from Priya's grasp, he ran into the house calling out for his father.

Hearing Ashok's frantic cries, his father came out of the study. His mother too hurried out of the kitchen.

"What is it, Ashok? Why are you shouting so loudly?" his father asked.

"Papa, Kumar is beating Chotu mercilessly. Please make him stop, Papa," Ashok panted. Papa did not wait to hear any more. He hurried out into the yard followed by Ashok and Ma.

"Stop it, Kumar!" Papa ordered. "Who gave you the right to beat a little boy like this?"

"Babuji, this boy has stolen the silver diya kept at the tulsi plant and refuses to tell me where he has hidden it,' Kumar replied, raising his hand to beat Chotu again. But

Papa held Kumar's hand. Chotu was clinging to Papa's feet crying, "Babuji, save me. I did not take the diya."

Before anyone could say anything more, Ma said, "But I took the diya. I thought it was too dirty and brought it in this morning to get it cleaned."

"Maji, it was you who t..t..took the diya?" Kumar stuttered.

"Yes. Whatever made you think that Chotu had taken it?" Ma demanded.

"I thought Chotu had stolen it," Kumar mumbled. "I am sorry, Maji. I never imagined that you might have taken it away."

"Next time be certain before you accuse anybody," Ma admonished. Kumar went away, looking quite sheepish.

Chotu was still sitting on the cobbled floor, nursing his sore cheek and sobbing. Ashok felt sorry for the little boy who was only about Priya's age.

"Don't cry, Chotu,' he said. "Nobody will ever beat you again."

"Does it hurt very badly, Chotu?" Priya asked. Chotu nodded, his cries having subsided to a whimper.

"Wait, I'll bring some lotion from Ma." Priya ran into the house. She soon returned with a bottle of lotion and applied it on Chotu's cheek. She wiped his tears with a towel she had picked up on the way out. Chotu looked at her adoringly. He thought Ashok and Priya were the nicest people he had ever met. He got up and giving them a watery grin, went off to do his work. Ashok and Priya went back into the house.

"Both of you have your bath and come down for breakfast," said Ma coming out of the kitchen as Ashok and Priya were going upstairs. "Asha has made your favourite dish."

"What has she made, Ma?" Priya asked.

"Hurry up and come down to the dining room and you will know," her mother said as she returned to the kitchen. The children ran upstairs. They hurried up with their washing and got ready.

Ashok put on a fresh white kurta and pajama while Priya chose a simple cotton frock in pink and white. As he buttoned up his kurta and combed his hair, Ashok kept yawning.

"I am so sleepy," he said, trying to stifle yet another yawn.

"Why? Didn't you sleep well last night?" asked Priya. "By the way, what time did you come up to bed? I waited quite a long time for you. Then I fell asleep and you hadn't returned."

It was only then that Ashok remembered all that had happened the night before. But before he could say anything Ma walked into the room, a glass in her hand.

"Who left this glass on the window sill last night?" she demanded. Ashok went red.

"I did, Ma. I felt thirsty and got up for a drink of water," he said.

"Did you also open the window?" Ma asked, her usually gentle face grim, her lips pressed together in a straight line.

"Yes, I did, Ma," Ashok mumbled. He remembered that he had not closed it before returning to his room.

"How many times have you been told not to open that window after dark?" Ma scolded. "You know that there is no grille there and anyone can climb up the pipe and get into the house. Why did you open it?"

"I forgot, Ma," Ashok apologised.

"That is not good enough," Ma said. "You are almost twelve years old, Ashok and old enough to realise what a risk it was to leave the window open. You could have put us all into grave danger. You know how much trouble there is in the city."

Ashok stood there looking foolish. He knew he had behaved irresponsibly. He apologised again and Ma went out of the room. Ashok and Priya followed her in silence.

They went and sat down at the dining table. Asha brought in two plates of hot aloo paranthas and bowls of thick cold yoghurt.

"Ooh, lovely!" Priya said, beginning on her parantha. Ashok's face too brightened.

"If only Asghar and Afshan were here," Priya said wistfully. "You know how much they love aloo paranthas."

Hearing this Asha, who was bringing fresh, steaming paranthas, laughed and said, "Well, why don't you use that *ghanti* (bell) to call them over?" She had been extremely amused at the contraption on which Ashok and Asghar had been working.

As she walked out of the room, Ashok said in a low voice. "Hurry up with your breakfast, Priya. I have lots to tell you." And he began eating his paranthas at top speed.

After breakfast, Ashok and Priya ran to their playroom, which was also their study. Nowadays they did their lessons with their father, as their regular tutor, Pandit Ram Saran Sharma, lived across the city and found it difficult to commute because of the disturbance in Delhi. In fact, the last time he had come he had told the children's father that he was planning to send his wife and children back to his village in the Himalayan foothills. He lived in a locality where most of his neighbours were Muslims and he feared for their lives, he said.

Ashok and Priya thought they would have no lessons till Pandit Sharma could come to teach them again. But their father dashed their hopes to the ground. Being a scholar himself, every morning and afternoon he taught them, keeping their noses to the grindstone.

The children got out their books and pencils in readiness for the morning's lessons. Ashok thought he would talk to his father about last night's events. Five minutes later, Papa walked in. But he appeared to be in a hurry.

"Children, today I will not be able to sit with you as I have to go somewhere with Srivastava Chacha," Papa said. "But I want you to study on your own. Ashok, I want to see that essay when I return. Priya, learn your multiplication tables and also revise your last geography lesson. Ashok, help Priya with her lessons," he added, buttoning up his starched kurta. He picked up his stout wooden cane and went out before Ashok could tell him anything.

Ashok waited for a few minutes. Soon he heard the front door close.

"Come on," he said, dragging Priya to the table where the "telephone" was set up. "I am going to try and call up Asghar. I must tell him all that has happened."

"But what has happened, Bhaiya?" Priya asked in a puzzled voice. "I don't know what you are talking about."

"You remember I went down to get my book? Just as I was leaving I found that the window was not shut properly. So I went to close it and I heard some voices in the lane outside. They were talking about some attack on the Khans.

But wait, let me ring up Asghar first. Then I will tell you all about it," Ashok said.

He began fiddling with the "telephone". At first, he could get no sound whatsoever. For all the response he got, the cans and wires might just as well not have been connected.

"What should I do?" Ashok muttered to himself. "After all, it did work yesterday evening." He pulled at this wire and that, pressed the switch, shifted certain other things, but all in vain. While he stood there wondering what to do next, Ma walked into the room. She was most annoyed to see that they had not even opened their books.

"Ashok! Priya! What are you doing at that table? Why haven't you begun on your lessons? You know Papa trusted you to work on your own. Come back to the study table at once!" Ma was really angry.

"Ma, I was trying to call up Asghar,' said Ashok. "Last night…" But Ma was in no mood to listen.

"I don't want to hear another word till you finish your lessons,' she said firmly and walked out of the room. Ashok looked at Ma's retreating back in frustration. Grown-ups could be so trying at times. Usually Papa and Ma were quite willing to hear what he and Priya had to say. But today both of them seemed distracted and too busy to pay them any attention.

Ashok sighed and opened his essay book. Uncapping his pen he wrote the title "My Country, My Motherland". Then he sat nibbling at his pen. He could not think of a single word to write. How he hated writing essays! He did not mind doing any amount of math, but essays were the bane of his existence.

He looked at Priya trying to memorise her tables. They were a real nightmare to her. She looked really funny—eyes closed, face all screwed up and her lips moving soundlessly as she tried to learn her multiplication tables. Ashok giggled. Priya opened her eyes and looked at him in surprise.

"What is wrong? What are you giggling at?" she asked.

"You looked so weird, your face all puckered up," Ashok gave a loud guffaw.

"Well, you had better laugh softly, Mr Smarty, or Ma will come in. Then you will be laughing with the other side of your face." Priya was indignant at being called weird. She tossed back her head of black curls and returned to her tables.

Ashok bent over his notebook and began on his essay. But half his mind was still on the "telephone" and the need to get in touch with Asghar. He kept stealing glances at the "telephone".

Once his essay was done, he returned to the array of wires and cans. Priya was still working at her lessons.

Quietly he started to fiddle with the wires again. He realised that one of the wires near the bell and the switch had come loose. He joined it again and fixed it with tape. Then he tried to contact Asghar again.

This time he was successful. At the first ring itself, Asghar picked up at the other end. Obviously he had been quite near the "telephone".

"Hello! Ashok?" he said.

"Listen Asghar, I have something urgent to tell you. Your family is in danger," said Ashok.

Priya left her books and paid attention to what Ashok was saying. Of course, she could not hear what Asghar was saying.

"Danger? What danger? Are you trying to pull my leg, Ashok?" Asghar asked in a suspicious voice.

"No Asghar, I am serious." Ashok's voice was urgent.

"Ok, what is it?" Asghar sounded puzzled.

"Last night I happened to hear something. Some people are plotting…" Ashok realised Priya was trying to tell him something.

"Somebody's coming," Priya whispered.

"Asghar, hang up for a minute. I will talk to you later. But don't go far from the 'telephone'. What I have to tell you is really important." Ashok put down the can and scampered back to the study table.

Not a minute too soon for Ma came in just then with a boy of about ten. Ashok mentally groaned at the sight of the boy. He was Ravi, a neighbour and one of the most unpopular boys in the locality.

"Children, Ravi came to borrow some flour. Talk to him while I go and bring it." Ma went out leaving Ravi behind.

Ravi was a pasty-faced boy with a thin, mean mouth and shifty eyes.

"What are you two doing?" he asked walking up to the table. "What goody-goody creatures. Studying even when your tutor has not come." His voice was mocking and Ashok went red.

"Studying is not being goody-goody. So what if Masterji doesn't come. Papa has been teaching us," he said.

"And anyway what business is it of yours whether we study or not?" Priya asked. She hated Ravi who was a bully. He always teased her. Now he pulled her hair and said, "Don't be rude. Remember I am your guest. I'll tell your mother you two were rude to me."

"Rotten sneak," said Ashok. "But you had better keep your hands to yourself or I'll punch you in the face." He looked so fierce that Ravi decided to leave Priya alone. He ambled to the table where the "telephone" was arranged.

"What is this?" he asked.

"Nothing," Ashok replied. "Just something I was playing with."

"But what are all these wires?" Ravi asked.

"Nothing. Don't fiddle with them, Ravi," Ashok said. He wished Ma would come soon so that Ravi could leave.

"I am not fiddling. But I want to know what you are trying to make. Tell me, Ashok," said Ravi.

"Then want will have to be your master," Ashok retorted. "And I told you to leave my things alone." He tried to pull Ravi away from the table. Ravi tried to pull back.

"What are both of you doing?" Ma asked walking into the room. "Ashok, let go of Ravi. I am ashamed of you, fighting with a guest." Ashok went red and let go of Ravi. Ravi fell backwards and clutched at the table for support. His fingers got entangled in the wires and all the cans, bells and switches fell off with a loud clatter.

Ma went to help Ravi get up. She brushed his shorts and said, "Here Ravi, take the flour to your mother." Giving Ashok a stern look she escorted Ravi out of the room.

Ashok and Priya stood looking at the mess on the floor, dismay writ large on their faces. Now what could they do? How would they contact Asghar?

**CHAPTER 4**
# A MYSTERIOUS CONVERSATION

Meanwhile what was happening at the Khans' house at the corner of the next street? Asghar sat in front of a table, which duplicated the arrangement on Ashok's. Here too were wires, cans, bells and switches. Yes, this was the other end of the "telephone".

Asghar's usually cheerful face wore a puzzled look, which did not go with his extremely youthful looks. Though the best of friends, Asghar and Ashok were as different from each other as chalk from cheese. Friends since the age of three, Ashok had always been tall and thin while Asghar was short and quite plump. However, in the last year or so Asghar had suddenly shot up so that he was now actually half a head taller than Ashok. As a result, he moved quite awkwardly as though he had not gotten used to his extra length yet. As he had also lost some of his puppy fat, his face had become more oval though there were still some remnants of his chubby looks, making him seem younger than his eleven years. Ashok was the more serious of the two and often acted as a brake on his friend's crazier exploits.

This morning Asghar sat before his "telephone" pondering over the weird conversation he had had with Ashok. He had seemed almost frantic. What could have happened to make him sound so worried? He wished Ashok would call again. He almost willed the bell on the table to ring.

Just then Afshan, his mischievous younger sister and Priya's alter ego, came into the room. Seeing her brother sitting in a trance, she said in a hoarse voice, "Bhaijaan, what are you thinking about?"

She was just recovering from a bad attack of flu and though her fever was down, her throat was still bad.

Asghar did not seem to hear, he was so lost in thought. Afshan, who was an incurable tease, began to badger him.

"Bhaijaan, don't think so hard or your brains will

collapse under the strain," she said in mock concern. "As it is you don't have all that much."

When he still did not retaliate she shook him and said, "Bhaijaan, Bhaijaan! Wake up! Tell me what is wrong? What has happened?"

This time she got through. Asghar had not even realised that Afshan had come into the room.

"What? What did you say?" he asked.

"What were you thinking about?" Afshan said. "You looked quite worried."

"Nothing really. Ashok had called up and he said…"

"Ashok called up? Bhaijaan, that means your 'telephone' works," Afshan shrieked. "That means I can talk to Priya. How I have missed her! Tell me how to operate it please, Bhaijaan."

"Hey, not so fast," said Asghar, laughing at her enthusiasm. "Yes, it does work, but it is not perfect by any means. We have to work on it much longer before it becomes a proper 'telephone'."

"Anyway tell me what Ashok said," Afshan said throwing herself into a cosy armchair. She was coughing by now.

"I could not really make out what he was saying. You see the volume keeps fluctuating and there is a lot of disturbance as well," said Asghar. "But he said something about a plot.

At first I thought he was pulling my leg. But he insisted he was extremely serious. He sounded quite worried. He said he would call again and I am waiting."

Just then the bell rang.

"That must be Ashok," Asghar said and grabbed the can. He kept it pressed to his ear for a couple of seconds and Afshan saw a puzzled expression cross his face.

"What's happened, Bhaijaan?" she asked, almost hopping with impatience.

"I don't know," Asghar replied, replacing the can on the table. "There was a crackling sound and then total silence. I think Ashok was trying to contact me but could not get through."

"What did Ashok say when he called earlier?" Afshan asked. She returned to her chair and curled up comfortably, tucking her feet under the cushion. She drew the light shawl lying on the chair around her.

"I don't know what exactly has happened," Asghar replied. "As I told you he mentioned some plot. It is quite clear that Ashok is worried about something and it involves us. But I can't believe that somebody would plot against us."

"I wonder," Afshan said.

Asghar gave her a surprised look. What could she mean? Then he remembered what he had read in the morning paper. Altogether thirty persons had been killed in the city in various places. But was his family in danger? No, it was not possible. His father was a very well liked man. Nobody would harm them, he was sure.

Meanwhile Ashok and Priya were discussing ways and means to somehow meet Asghar and Afshan.

"What can we do?" Priya asked her brother, biting her nails in anxiety. "We won't be allowed to go out of the house, that is certain."

"Certainly not after today's newspaper report," Ashok agreed.

"What did it say, Bhaiya?" Priya asked.

"It said that more than thirty people were killed in the city yesterday and that there was a possibility of more violence today," Ashok said. "However, Mahatma Gandhi has gone on fast again and refuses to eat anything till people stop killing each other."

"I hope people listen to Bapu at least," said Priya. Both fell silent after that, each lost in their own thoughts.

Ashok was going over all that he had heard through the open window last night. Those people certainly had it in for the Khans. Then he remembered what that man named Vishnu had said. He wanted to get even with Mr Khan for dismissing him from his job or something. Well, Vishnu at least was not doing anything for his religion, but because he had a personal score to settle. What Ma said was true. No true Hindu or Muslim would kill in the name of religion.

Priya stood at the window looking at the empty lane outside. It was here that Ashok had stood when he heard those men talking in the lane. How could she help Afshan? Had she recovered from her fever? How horrible it would be if something happened to her or her family. If only she could slip across to Afshan's house and warn her to be careful. But how could she? Then she saw the stain of flour on the windowsill. Ma had kept the packet there when she had gone to help Ravi get up and brush him down after his fall. Thinking about Ravi, how did he get here? She turned to Ashok.

"Bhaiya!" she called. "Bhaiya, Bhaiya!" Priya called louder.

"Yes, what is it?" Ashok asked jerking himself out of his thoughts.

"Bhaiya, how did Ravi manage to get here? After all, his house is not all that near," said Priya.

"I don't know," said Ashok, a wondering look on his face. "Ravi would have had to cross the big ground and then the main road to come here."

"Just what I thought," said Priya. "And if Ravi could come here, we can go to Afshan's."

Priya sounded quite excited.

"I don't know, but you may be right," said Ashok brightening up. "Come on, let's go and ask Ma." Both of them ran out in search of their mother.

Ma was in her room arranging the cupboard. She turned around at the sound of running feet, her arms full of clothes. As Priya and Ashok came to a stop in front of her, panting from their wild run up the stairs, she asked, "Have you two finished all the work Papa gave you to do?"

"Yes Ma," Ashok replied.

"Ma, can we go to Asghar and Afshan's house?" Priya asked.

"No, darling, it is not safe to go out," Ma replied, turning back to the cupboard.

"But Ravi came here and nothing happened to him," Ashok pointed out.

"But that was different. They had no flour at all in their house and with curfew in most parts of the city, they could not buy any either. You know his father is out of station and he and his mother are all alone at home. So his mother sent Ravi here," explained Ma. "He had to sneak through the hedge to the house at the end of the lane and then creep up to our house. And he came and knocked at the backdoor."

"Well, Ma, may I go to Asghar's and come back? Priya can stay here and I promise not to be away too long," Ashok pleaded.

"No, Ashok, I am sorry I can't let you do that," said Ma. "Papa has said that none of us must even venture out. Once the trouble in the city dies down you can go to Asghar's for as long as you want. Asghar and Afshan are not running away, are they?"

Ashok's pleas fell on deaf ears. Ma was firm. She refused to let either of them go. Ashok wondered whether he should tell Ma all that had happened the night before. Maybe then she would agree to let them go to Asghar's.

"Ma, I want to tell you something," began Ashok. "Last night…." But before he could say anything more, Asha walked in.

"Maji, Sudhaji is waiting for you downstairs," she said.

"Is she already here? I had better hurry," said Ma, locking up the cupboard. "Children, I am going for a meeting. Be good till I return."

And she hurried out of the room. Ashok and Priya looked at each other.

"What are we going to do now?" Priya asked.

"I am going to Asghar's house somehow," said Ashok, a most determined look on his face.

"But how are you going to manage it, Bhaiya?" Priya asked.

"I will do it somehow," Ashok replied. "I can't just sit here and do nothing after what I heard last night."

"What did you hear exactly, Bhaiya? You haven't yet told me what happened last night," Priya said.

"Yes, so much has happened since that I did not get a chance to do so," said Ashok. "I told you that when I went downstairs to pick up my book I heard some people talking on the road. I was about to leave when I heard them mention Khan Chacha's name. From what I heard I gathered that they plan to attack the Khans at midnight. One of their men is working at the Khans as a servant and he will let them in. So now you know how important it is that I somehow warn Asghar."

Priya had been looking more and more worried as Ashok narrated his story. Now she said, "But how will you go to Asghar's house, Bhaiya?"

"I will go after it is dark," Ashok replied.

"But suppose Ma and Papa come to know?"

"I'll go at about nine o'clock tonight," Ashok said. "Ma will make me go to bed early to punish me for wandering about last night. So I can easily slip away. Papa will be reading in his study and Ma will be busy in the kitchen. Nobody will miss me."

"I'll also come with you," Priya said.

"If we both go off there is bound to be trouble," said Ashok. "There is a higher possibility of Ma or Papa coming to know."

"But if Ma asks where you are I can't lie to her," Priya said.

"Nobody is asking you to lie, silly. All you have to do is give an evasive reply. I will arrange my pillow to seem as though I am sleeping on my bed. Perhaps it will be a good idea if you too go to bed early. Then if Ma or Papa come into the room to ask any uncomfortable questions, you can pretend to be fast asleep."

Priya agreed, though reluctantly, and both she and Ashok went into the garden. They flung themselves on the *durrie* (cotton rug) spread out under the neem tree.

"Bhaiya, suppose those men are planning to attack Asghar's family tonight?" Priya asked. "After all they only said midnight and not which day, did they?"

"No, they didn't," said Ashok.

"Well, then if they plan to attack tonight then nine o'clock would be too late, wouldn't it?"

Ashok was in a quandary. What Priya said was true. So what could he do now?

"If only I could find out who Vishnu is," he said.

"Vishnu? Who is Vishnu?" Priya asked.

"One of the men was called Vishnu," said Ashok. "And he seemed to be the gang leader. If I could find out who he is I am sure I could somehow find out exactly when they plan to attack the Khans."

Suddenly they heard a rustling from a bush nearby. They looked at each other. Who could it be? Was someone spying on them?

"Who is there?" Ashok called, a tremble in his voice betraying his anxiety.

"It is I," said a voice and Chotu appeared from behind the bush.

"What were you doing behind the bush, Chotu?" Ashok asked in surprise.

"I wasn't behind the bush, Ashok Bhaiya. I was inside it," Chotu replied in a timid voice.

"Inside the bush? What do you mean?" Ashok asked.

"Come, I'll show you," Chotu parted the thick bush at a side and revealed his hiding place. The centre of the bush was hollow providing enough space for a child to sit or lie down. The ground was covered with dry leaves preventing the dampness from creeping through and once inside no one would be able to see the hidden person.

"I come here quite often when I am free and don't want Kumar to find me," Chotu explained.

Just then they heard Kumar shouting for Chotu. In a trice the little boy squeezed in through the leaves and was hidden from sight.

"Have you seen Chotu, Ashok Baba?" Kumar asked, coming round the neem tree.

"Yes, we have," replied Ashok.

"Then where is he? Do you think I should shout louder for him?"

"Well, I am sure he can hear you," said Ashok. Thinking how close Chotu really was, Priya gave a giggle which she turned into a cough.

"I think I had better go somewhere else and search for him," said Kumar, walking away. As soon as he was out of sight, Chotu emerged from the bush.

"Bhaiya, I could not help but hear what you and Priya were talking about earlier," said Chotu, dusting the dry leaves off his clothes. "Were you referring to Vishnu Verma who has a pock-marked face and only one eye?" he asked.

"I don't know,' Ashok replied. "I have only heard his voice. I have never seen him. But I know he used to work for Khan Chacha."

"Yes, that is Vishnu Verma," Chotu said. "He worked as a cashier at the Khans' shoe factory. I heard Kumar tell Asha that Vishnu had stolen money and was dismissed. When he left he made an ugly scene and vowed to revenge himself on Khan Sahab."

"That explains it," Ashok muttered, remembering the venom in Vishnu's voice. He looked at Chotu who seemed to want to say something more but seemed reluctant. "What is it Chotu?" Ashok asked gently.

"Ashok Bhaiya, I heard you talk about the attack on the Khans," said Chotu. "I think I can tell you when the attack will take place." Ashok and Priya looked at Chotu in surprise.

"How do you know?" Ashok asked.

"When is it to be?" asked Priya.

"When I went to throw out the garbage last night Vishnu and his friends were standing under a tree and talking. They did not see me and I heard them talking about an attack," said Chotu. "I did not pay much attention but I heard them say that tomorrow night would be ideal as it would be Amavasya and so there would be no moon."

Ashok was trembling with excitement. He thumped Chotu on the back and said: "Good boy! You don't know what a help you have been." Just then they heard Kumar shouting for Chotu and he ran away.

"Bhaiya, now it is all right," said Priya. "You can go and warn Asghar tonight and they can be ready to nab the intruders when they come to attack them."

"Yes. It was a piece of luck that Chotu happened to overhear our conversation," Ashok agreed, his eyes alight with excitement. He could hardly wait for the night to descend on the city.

**CHAPTER 5**

# A WALK IN THE NIGHT

Dinner was a quiet meal that night. Papa's friend, Bhawani Shankar, was there and both he and Papa seemed lost in their thoughts. They had had to be dragged in to dinner and as soon as the meal was over, they retired to the baithak again.

Bhawani Chacha was a serious person, little given to jokes and laughter, and Ashok and Priya were in awe of him.

Once dinner was over, Ashok and Priya went to their own room. They were both excited, but were trying their best not to show it.

"When are you planning to leave, Bhaiya?" Priya asked. "It is past eight now."

"I will leave soon after nine," replied Ashok. They heard voices in the hall and peeped out. Bhawani Chacha was leaving.

"Okay, Gupta, remember all that we talked about," said Bhawani Chacha.

"Don't worry, I won't forget anything," said Papa. He shut the door behind Bhawani Chacha and not only locked and bolted it, but dragged the huge table against it as well. Priya and Ashok looked at each other. Obviously Papa feared something.

"Bhaiya, do you think it is safe for you to go?" Priya asked, her voice trembling with fear.

"Don't worry. Nothing will happen to me," Ashok reassured her. He looked up and down the corridor. He could hear Papa rustling his newspaper and Ma talking to Asha in the kitchen. He dragged Priya further into the room and said, "Priya, let us go to the baithak."

"What for, Bhaiya?" she asked in surprise.

"We'll go and read our books there." Ashok said. "But you must keep yawning so that Papa sends us to bed."

"But I am not sleepy," Priya protested.

"I know, stupid," said Ashok. "But Ma seems to have forgotten that I am supposed to go to bed an hour early. If

I offer to go she is bound to think I am sickening for something and will begin to fuss. But if we yawn then Papa will send us to bed. And if we are supposed to be in bed, then there is less chance of my being missed. I can easily slip out then."

They picked up their storybooks and went to the baithak. Everything went according to plan. They settled down near Papa for a read. Priya kept yawning her head off till Papa said in an irritated voice, "Why don't you two go to bed?" To his surprise both of them jumped up with alacrity and went off upstairs. He looked at them, a thoughtful expression on his face.

Ashok waited for about fifteen minutes. Priya had changed and was in bed. They had arranged the pillows on Ashok's bed so that at first sight it looked as though somebody was asleep.

"Well, Priya, remember what I said. Stall any questions from Ma and I will try to be back as soon as possible."

"But how are you going to leave the house, Bhaiya?" Priya asked. "You saw how Papa has almost barricaded the front door."

"Yes, but I am going out through the backdoor," Ashok replied.

Once he felt the coast was clear, he crept out of the room and ran downstairs on tiptoes.

He first went to the small room where Chotu slept and called to the little boy.

"Chotu, come and lock up after me. I am going to Asghar's house," he whispered.

The two of them walked silently to the backdoor and opened it carefully. Ashok slipped out and Chotu locked it after him.

Ashok ran across the yard to the small gate in the corner and jumped over it. He did not dare open it as it sometimes creaked. He found himself in the lane and keeping to the side of the wall, soon reached the road.

The road was deserted. Remembering what it had been like before, Ashok felt quite sad.

At this time of the evening usually there would be people strolling about, taking their after-dinner walk. On summer nights there would be groups of children standing and chatting or sitting on the stone parapet, which lined both sides of the road, playing *antakshri*.

But all that gaiety and joy had vanished and only a heavy silence was left in the wake of the senseless violence that had rocked the city. How Ashok wished those days would return.

This was no time for nostalgia, however. He had more important things to do. He hid behind a huge neem tree and waited a few minutes. He peered into the darkness.

There was no moon and it was pitch dark. There seemed to be no one about. It should be safe to venture out into the lane.

He came out from behind the tree and ran softly down the lane. He wore rubber-soled shoes and made no sound whatsoever. Once he reached the end of the lane, he crouched in the shadows of a tall hedge. He had to turn the corner and go to the row of houses down the next lane. This was a dangerous part for he would be out in the open and in full view for a few minutes.

He peered round the corner cautiously. To his shock, he saw a huge bulk standing there. He quickly withdrew into his dark corner.

Who was it? Heavens! That was close! The man coughed and cleared his throat softly. Ashok heaved a sigh of relief.

He would know that cough anywhere. It was Khan Chacha's guard, Jumman. He was about to call out to him when he remembered the conversation he had heard last night. Those men had talked of Ramu being sent as a servant to Khan Chacha's house. So could he trust Jumman? But Jumman was such a nice person. On the other hand, Ramu would have to an extremely good actor to take in Khan Chacha who was said to be quite a shrewd person. No, he had better not take any risk whatsoever. Ashok stayed quiet till he heard Jumman move away.

He waited a few minutes more and then quickly ran round the corner. Once he was in the lane leading to Khan Chacha's house, he felt safer. Keeping to the shadows, he reached Asghar's garden. He crept in through a hole in the hedge. So far he had been lucky. He knelt down behind a jasmine bush and waited. The bush was full of blooms and the perfume was quite heady.

Ashok could make out the wires he and Asghar had connected for their so-called "telephone". It was attached to the wall and went across the terrace and down the wall at the back of the house, as it was the shortest route. But it was sagging and looked quite ugly. They would have to find some way of making it taut and unobtrusive. Ashok waited to make sure that no one was about and then ran softly to the window of Asghar's room.

The Khans' house was a low rambling bungalow. Afshan and Asghar's playroom was at one corner almost in a wing by itself. Ashok crouched beneath the window, wondering whether he should knock. He raised his hand to tap on the glass when he suddenly froze. He heard someone moving about in the room. Then he grinned to himself in the dark. How dumb of him! His nerves were all on edge. Of course, it must be Asghar in the room. He tapped lightly on the window.

Just after that he remembered that at this time of the

night it was most unlikely that Asghar would be in his playroom. The Khans always had early dinner and most probably Asghar was in his bedroom at the other end of the house. Now what could he do? He quickly ran to a rose bush close by and ducked behind it.

Not a minute too soon either, for the window was opened cautiously and a face peeped out. Ashok could not make out who it was. It was too dark. Luckily just then a patrol guard flashed his torch around and the face was caught in the flash of light before the man ducked back into the room. That glimpse was enough for Ashok. He had recognised the face. It belonged to Yusuf, one of the children's favourites among Khan Chacha's servants. He was very friendly and often joined in their games.

Ashok was just about to rise and call out when he heard Yusuf ask in a loud whisper: "Who is it? Vishnu?"

Ashok's heart missed a beat. Why was Yusuf calling for Vishnu? Vishnu was an enemy of the Khans while Yusuf was a friend. So what was the link between the two men?

Suddenly an idea struck him. He remembered the conversation he had heard last night. What was it again? What had that man said? "That was a good idea of yours, Vishnu, to ask Ramu to get into the house as a servant."

Suddenly everything seemed to fall into place.

Yusuf was the servant, Ramu, the men had been talking

about. Ashok felt his hands turn clammy. Yusuf, an enemy? He felt a bitter taste in his mouth. Was there nobody one could trust in this world now? How stupid of him! Of course, there were. He could trust Asghar with his life.

Again Yusuf's voice was heard. "Is anyone there?" Ashok crouched lower behind the bush. Receiving no reply, Yusuf withdrew into the room and shut the window.

After waiting for a few minutes, which seemed hours to the impatient Ashok, he came out of his hiding place and crept round the house keeping close to the wall.

Soon he reached the window of Asghar's bedroom. The light was on. This he could make out through the gap in the curtains. He tried to peep in but the gap was not wide enough. Suddenly he heard a rustling in the bushes nearby. He stayed still. Who could it be? To his relief a stray cat emerged from the bushes and ran across the garden.

Cautiously, Ashok raised his head and tried to peep through the window. Luckily the curtains fluttered in the breeze from the ceiling fan and the chink between them became wide enough to allow Ashok a glimpse of the room. Asghar was alone in the room. He was sprawled on the chair reading.

Ashok tapped softly on the windowpane.

Asghar had been lost in the mystery novel when the tapping jerked him back to the present. He looked up from his book in surprise. What was that noise? It sounded as though someone was tapping at his window. He looked at the clock on his bedside table. It was half past nine. Who could it be?

He got up and went to the window. He opened it a crack.

"Psst! Asghar!" Ashok hissed. Recognising Ashok's voice, Asghar opened the window wider, a startled look on his face.

"What are you...," Asghar began, but Ashok shushed him immediately.

"Ssssh! Let me in," he whispered.

Asghar helped Ashok climb in through the window. As Ashok jumped down from the windowsill they heard the sound of footsteps in the corridor.

"I think somebody is coming. It is important that no one knows that I am here. Where can I hide?" Ashok asked in an urgent whisper.

"Crawl under the bed," Asghar suggested. Ashok ran to the bed and crawled under it pulling down the bedcover after him. Not a minute too soon for just then somebody knocked on the door.

"Come in," said Asghar, and watched the door open slowly. Who could be coming to his room at this time of the night?

## CHAPTER 6
# THE PLAN

Mr Bhawani Shankar walked down the road from the Guptas' house. The road was quite empty. His thoughts were quite similar to those in Ashok's mind when he had walked the same road half an hour later. Mr Shankar too lamented the passing of a peaceful period.

But whereas Ashok longed to go back to that time, Mr Shankar did not. For despite all the troubles that followed in the wake of partition of the country into India and Pakistan, Mr Shankar could not help but rejoice at having thrown off the chains of bondage. At last, after

200 years, India was free.

Mr Shankar remembered how much he and many like him all over the country had suffered to get this freedom from the British. He remembered how he had to run from British bullets and the innumerable blows from lathis while demonstrating non-violently against a foreign dictator. No, he never wanted to go back to a life of bondage.

He reached Mr Srivastava's house. He knocked softly on the door. There was no response. So he knocked a bit louder. This time he heard footsteps approaching the door. Then he heard Mr Srivastava call out, "Who is there?"

"Open up Srivastava, it is Bhawani," Mr Shankar said. He heard the sound of bolts being drawn back and the door opened to let him in.

"I was waiting for you," Mr Srivastava said, bolting the door again. "Did you meet Gupta? Is he coming?"

"Yes, I am coming from his house," said Mr Shankar. "He said he will not be here for the meeting, but will meet us here at half past eleven."

"Well, let us go to the study," said Mr Srivastava, leading the way. "Chatterjee is already here."

Soon they reached the study where a man dressed in police uniform was sprawled on the sofa. "Come in, my dear Bhawani, you sure took a long time coming," he greeted Mr Shankar. "Where were you, my friend?"

"I was with Gupta. I had dinner there and then came straight here. How come you could leave the station, Chatterjee?"

"Well, I have an able deputy," said Mr Chatterjee. "And anyway I have to go back. So let us finalise the details quickly."

"Yes, let us do so," said Mr Srivastava, dragging his chair closer to the sofa.

"We have already decided to meet here at half past eleven," said Mr Shankar. "I think it was a really good idea to form a neighbourhood watch committee to patrol the area. Well, as it is our turn, Gupta and I will patrol the neighbourhood tonight. At one o' clock I will come along to the station and give you a report. Is that alright?"

"Yes, that is okay." said Mr Chatterjee. "The only thing is I will be going home at midnight. So if I am not there, just tell my deputy, Aslam. He knows all about our patrolling scheme. So it will be okay."

"But suppose we need reinforcements?" asked Mr Shankar.

"Don't worry. I won't be taking the jeep. So one of the hawaldars can come and pick me up if needed. I have left all instructions with Aslam," Mr Chatterjee replied.

"Right, I will do that," Mr Shankar said. "I'll make a

move now. I'll see you, Srivastava, in about two hours. So long, Chatterjee."

"I'll also make tracks for the police station," said Mr Chatterjee, getting up. "See you later, Srivastava."

Both Mr Shankar and Mr Chatterjee left Mr Srivastava's house and walked off in opposite directions. The street was silent once more.

# CHAPTER 7
# SUDDEN DISCOVERY

After Ashok left, Priya lay in bed, wondering and worrying. What could Ashok be doing? She had switched off the light and lay in darkness fearing that if she left the light on, someone might come to inquire and then all would be lost. Now even if Ma came upstairs, she could pretend to be asleep and, with luck, Ma would think Ashok was also fast asleep on his bed.

But Priya could not sleep. She lay in bed going over all that had happened. Were she and Ashok making a mountain of a molehill? Or was Asghar's family in real danger? It was lucky that Chotu had heard that conversation near the garbage dump. Otherwise there was no way they could have found out when the troublemakers were planning to attack the Khans. Now, Ashok should be able to get to Asghar's house and warn them in time.

She turned to the other side and looked towards the window. The shutters were wide open to let in the cool night air. Usually the moonlight fell right on her face. But tonight there was no moon. It was pitch dark.

Suddenly she sat up. There was something that was disturbing her. Something that Chotu had said. It did not ring right. But what was it?

She went over what Chotu had told them. He had heard the men say that tomorrow night was the right time to attack the Khans as it was Amavasya and there would be no moon. In the darkness it would be easier to slink off.

She looked at the sky through the window. The next moment she jumped out of bed and ran to the window. There was no moon.

Heavens, what idiots they had been. Tonight was Amavasya! The attack was supposed to take place tonight. But, of course! Chotu had heard the conversation last night. Their tomorrow was today!

Now not only were the Khans in danger, but Ashok as well. Priya switched on her torch and flashed it at the clock on the table. It was half past nine. Ashok must be at Asghar's house by now.

Priya wiped her brow. She was sweating though the night was not so hot. What could she do? Should she tell Ma and Papa? Yes, she had better. It was too serious for her to deal with on her own.

She went out of her room and ran downstairs to the baithak. She could see the light shining under the door so obviously Papa was still up. She ran to the door and banged on it calling out loudly all the while.

"Priya baba, what is wrong? Why are you making so much noise," Asha asked, coming from the dining room. "What is the matter?"

"Asha, where are Ma and Papa?" demanded Priya. "Quick, I must talk to them just now." Her voice trembled with urgency and fear.

"I don't know, Priya baba. I was busy in the kitchen when someone knocked on the door. Your Papa opened the door. Then Maji came and told me they had to go out and I should lock the door," Asha said. "Why? What is wrong?" Seeing Priya's face, she added, "Come into the room and tell me what has happened."

Priya was in a daze. Now what was she to do? She could not explain everything to Asha. After all, what could Asha do? It was the first time that Priya had had to deal with something like this and that too on her own. So far, Ashok had always been there for her to turn to.

Asha sat Priya down in the armchair and gave her a glass of water.

"Drink that up and then tell me what is wrong," she repeated. Priya gulped down her sobs and drank the water. She felt slightly calmer.

"It is nothing, Asha, just something that I had to tell Papa. I just hope they will return soon. Did they tell you when they would be back?"

"No, Priya Baba, Maji did not tell me anything. She just told me to sleep in the hallway so that I would hear as soon as they knocked. And Maji did not change her salwar-kameez so I think she went somewhere nearby," Asha replied.

She looked quite worried at Priya's questions.

"Don't worry, Asha. I'll wait up till they return. Just call me as soon as Ma and Papa come back." Priya left the room, followed by Asha who switched off the light and shut the door.

Asha went back to the kitchen to finish the washing-up. She was tired and longed for bed.

Priya went up the stairs. She knew she would not be able to sleep till Ashok returned safely. But she could lie down on her bed quietly. As she reached the top landing she saw Chotu coming down carrying the dirty clothes for the next day's laundry. He smiled at her adoringly.

"Where is Ashok Bhaiya? I wanted to show him a funny insect I caught in the garden today. I know how fond he is of insects. I have kept it in a box…" His voice petered out as he noticed the expression on Priya's face. "What is wrong? You look as though you have been crying," he said, putting the basket of clothes on the top stair.

"Oh Chotu, I am so scared," said Priya, a sob rising in her throat at the thought of the danger that was threatening Ashok. "We all thought tomorrow was the night that Vishnu and the others planned to attack the Khans. But Amavasya is tonight. And Ashok Bhaiya has gone to warn Asghar. I don't know what will happen to him." She could not control her tears any more and ran to her room.

Chotu sat down beside the basket on the stairs. He was stunned. He had thought he was helping Ashok Bhaiya. But all he had done was send him straight into danger. What would happen now? Would Ashok Bhaiya also be hurt? He wished he could do something.

"Chotu! Oh Chotu! How much longer are you…," called Asha as she came out of the kitchen. "Are you sitting here? And I have been waiting for you to come in to switch off the kitchen light."

"I was just coming," mumbled Chotu and carried the basket of dirty clothes through the kitchen to the yard at the back where Ram Pyari, the washerwoman, would wash it the next morning. He soaked the clothes in the big bucket of warm soapy water that Asha had prepared. He looked up at the sky. It was pitch dark. Priya was right. It was Amavasya tonight.

What a fool he had been not to realise that. Now he came to think about it he remembered Asha and Ram Pyari talking that morning. They had said they would have to take a bath before going to bed as it was Amavasya.

Chotu cursed himself for his oversight. Suddenly he got an idea. Why shouldn't he slip along to the Khans' house and warn Ashok Bhaiya? It must be about ten o'clock as Asha had only just finished her work. She usually went to bed by half past. So that meant he had ample time to warn Ashok Bhaiya.

He trembled with fear at the thought of walking alone on the road in the dark. But he gave himself a mental shake and decided to be brave. After all, if it hadn't been for Ashok Bhaiya, Kumar would have beaten him black and blue over the missing diya. Walking down the road on a dark night to save Ashok Bhaiya from danger was something that he had to do. He should be brave, he told himself.

"Chotu, come in and lock the door," Asha called out. Chotu hurried back into the house, locking the door to the yard behind him.

He went into the tiny room off the kitchen and spread out his sleeping mat on the floor. He heard Asha switch off the kitchen light and go to her room off the back verandah. Now it should be safe to get up and leave the house.

Just as he was leaving the room he heard Asha returning. He was surprised. Why was she coming back? He peeped out carefully. He saw Asha go towards the hallway, her sheet under her arm. Why was she going to sleep in the hall, he wondered.

That meant he could not go out the front door.

But that wasn't a problem actually. He could as easily leave through the backdoor.

He waited till he was sure that Asha would have settled down and then he slipped out of his room.

He crept out the backdoor, just as Ashok had done a little over an hour earlier. He too jumped over the gate so that it would not creak and give him away.

Out in the lane, he felt a shiver of fear. It was so dark and lonely. Not a soul stirred. His heart thudding painfully, he ran on bare feet down the road.

At the corner, he too waited behind the neem tree. As he stood there he heard the sound of footsteps. They seemed to be coming from the same direction that he had come. He had better move to the other side of the tree. But just then he heard more footsteps approaching from the other direction. Now what was he to do?

He had to decide in a hurry. The footsteps were coming closer every second. In a trice, he climbed up the tree and hid among the thick foliage.

He heard the footsteps come to a stop below the tree. Thank God he had decided to climb up the tree. If he had been on the ground, he would have been caught by the men.

He carefully parted the leaves and looked down. Two men were standing there. They were standing very still, not even talking to each other.

"How long are they going to stand here?" Chotu wondered.

He was developing cramps. He shifted himself a bit, taking care not to make any noise. Ah, that was better. The branch was quite wide and Chotu lay down more comfortably. Almost before he knew it, the small boy had fallen asleep.

He never heard anything. The little boy was tired and he would have continued to sleep till the morning except for an owl that had made a nest in the same tree. The owl was not very happy at Chotu sharing its tree and hooted loudly near his ear. Chotu woke up suddenly and for a moment wondered where he was. Then he remembered everything. Gosh, how could he have fallen asleep like that?

He peered down from the tree. There was no one there. Who were the men? Why had they come there?

He felt ashamed of himself. He felt he had betrayed Ashok and Priya. Heaven knew what the time was. Just then the police station clock struck the half-hour. It was 11.30 PM. He was grateful to the owl for having woken him up. Well, he couldn't delay any longer. He had better hurry up and run to Asghar's house.

# CHAPTER 8
# EXCITING NIGHT

Meanwhile what was happening at Asghar's house? When the door opened fully, Asghar drew a breath of relief. It was only Afshan.

"Gosh, you gave me a shock. What do you want?" Asghar asked.

"Nothing. I just wanted to borrow your book. Have you finished it?" Afshan said.

Then she noticed how tense he was. "What is wrong, Bhaijaan?"

"Come in and shut the door, and I will tell you." She

did as he said and sat down on the chair.

"Okay, now tell me," she invited. But before Asghar could say anything Ashok came out from under the bed. Her mouth fell open in surprise. "When did you…" she began in a loud voice.

Both boys immediately shut her up. "Quieten down, will you? You will have everyone here if you shriek like that," Asghar said.

"Okay. But tell me what are you doing here, Ashok Bhaiya?" she asked in a softer voice.

"I came here to warn you," Ashok replied.

"Warn us? What about?" asked Afshan.

"Some people plan to hurt you. They have planned the attack for midnight tomorrow," Ashok said.

"Are you sure, Ashok? How do you know all this?" Afshan asked. "Are you sure this is not from one of those mystery stories that you like to read?"

"No, you have to believe me. And we have to quickly decide what to do?" Ashok said.

Hearing the note of urgency in Ashok's voice, Asghar spoke up.

"OK, fine. But first you had better tell us how you learnt about this," he said.

Ashok quickly told the brother and sister all that he had overheard and what Chotu had overheard as well.

"So you see, at first, we didn't know when the attack was to happen. I had only heard the men say that they would attack you at midnight, not on which day. But luckily Chotu overheard some men talking about an attack on Amavasya night tomorrow. I wanted to come to you earlier, but Ma wouldn't let me. So I sneaked out when I was supposed to be in bed and here I am. Now I had better go or Priya will be getting worried," Ashok said.

He ran to the window and opened it. Just as he was about to climb out, Asghar stopped him.

"Wait, Ashok. I think someone is coming. You had better hide," he whispered.

Ashok slid under the bed and lay as quiet as a mouse.

There was a knock on the door.

"Come in," Asghar called out, trying to stop his voice from trembling. He was still in shock after all that Ashok had told him.

Ashok heard the slight quiver in his friend's voice and felt a stab of anger at those who were responsible for it. How dare a few people scare so many, forcing them to live in fear? Especially nice people like Asghar and Afshan who had never done any harm to anyone.

He heard someone come into the room. He peeped from under the bed. But all he could see was a pair of broad feet. Then the person spoke and Ashok's eyes widened in alarm. It was Yusuf who had come in. He wanted to warn Asghar and Afshan not to let out anything to Yusuf.

When he had related the whole story to them he had not named Yusuf. He had only told them that one of the plotters had entered their household as a servant.

"Why aren't you children in bed?" Ashok heard Yusuf ask. "Your Ammi will be very annoyed if you don't go to sleep soon. And Afshan, what are you doing here? Didn't Ammi say you should go to bed early? You know you still haven't recovered fully from your illness."

"Yes, Yusuf, I was just going," said Afshan. "I just came here to get a book from Bhaijaan. That was when…"

"Oh no, now she will tell Yusuf everything," Ashok said to himself.

But just then he heard her exclaim: "Ouch, Bhaijaan, that hurt. Why did you do that?"

"I am sorry Afshan, but I was just giving you the book that you wanted. Now take it and go. Stop troubling me. You are a real pest," said Asghar.

"Bhaijaan, I…I…I…," Afshan stuttered in surprise.

"Asghar Baba, you should not treat your younger sister like that. Suppose the book had hit her in the face or something? Luckily it only hit her on her hand. I think I will have to tell your Ammi," Yusuf said.

"I am sorry, Yusuf. But I wanted to sleep and she has

been pestering me. And now Ammi will scold me for not going to bed when it is all actually her fault. Anyway I will apply some lotion on her arm and then send her to her room. You can go, Yusuf," Asghar said.

To Ashok's relief, Yusuf left the room.

He came out from under the bed and found Afshan nursing her arm on which was a red mark where Asghar's book had hit her. Her eyes were full of tears and she looked at her brother in bewilderment.

"I am sorry, Afshan but I couldn't think of any other way of stopping you from telling Yusuf about Ashok and his message," Asghar said.

"But what is wrong in telling Yusuf? He is our friend," said Afshan.

"But Ashok said one of the plotters was in our house. How do we know who that is?" said Asghar, bringing a bottle of lotion from the cupboard and applying it gently on his sister's arm.

"I don't think that is Yusuf. Have you forgotten how he plays with us and is always taking us out for treats and so on?" Afshan said.

"However, Asghar is right, Afshan. I forgot to tell you, but the men spoke about Yusuf by name," said Ashok. "His real name is Ramu. He is an orphan and he was brought up by Muslim foster parents. That is why no one could guess that he was not a Muslim."

"And we have been so trusting. How could he do this? Pretend to be our friend and then plot against us?" Asghar said.

"I think Vishnu must have promised him a lot of money. Otherwise why would he join them?" Ashok said.

"You are right, Ashok Baba. How clever of you to deduce that," said a voice from the doorway.

The children turned around to see Yusuf standing there. But this was a very different Yusuf from the one they knew. Gone was the friendly demeanour, the big smile. This one was a frightening person with cold eyes and thin lips that didn't have even the trace of a smile.

He came into the room quickly and shut the door and locked it.

"I am sorry that you had to get involved in this, Ashok. But now we have no choice, but to kill you with your friends. At least, you will all be together till the end," he said with a harsh laugh.

"But Yusuf, you are our friend," Afshan said, her voice trembling with tears.

"Yes, I was. But I need the money to buy my house back from the moneylender in the village. And Vishnu has promised to give it to me if I help him tonight," Yusuf said.

Asghar was furious. To think that someone whom he

had trusted so much should agree to destroy his family just for some money. He rushed at Yusuf. But Yusuf was too quick for him. He pulled Afshan to him and whipped out a knife.

"You had better stay where you are, Asghar. Or your sister will be the first of your family to die," he said, holding an ugly knife at Afshan's throat.

Asghar and Ashok stood absolutely still. Yusuf took some rope and tied Afshan's hands together. Then he took her scarf and gagged her mouth. Then he did the same to the two boys.

"Now I will leave you here in the darkened room and lock it up. No one will come in as they think you are asleep. I will come for you once the others come in at midnight. Goodnight!"

With another harsh laugh he switched off the light and went out of the room.

The children lay there silently in the darkness. They couldn't even whisper to each other because of the gags.

Each was thinking his own thoughts.

So it was tonight that the attacks were planned for. Of course, now that he remembered what Chotu had said, he realised what a fool he had been not to have guessed. Chotu had heard the conversation last night and the men had said the attack would be tomorrow. Of course, that meant today. Ashok felt like kicking himself.

But he was not going to give in without a fight. He tried to think how he could escape from this situation.

Asghar was feeling frustrated, frightened and angry. But most of all he was angry. He couldn't understand how some men could so heartlessly talk of killing someone. And that too someone who had been so kind to them like his father. He remembered how Abba had given Yusuf money when he had wanted to go to his village when his mother had died.

That must have been a lie actually as Ashok said that Yusuf or Ramu as he was actually called, was an orphan. And his Ammi had given Yusuf new clothes for Eid as he had hardly any good clothes. Both Abba and Ammi had been so happy at the way Yusuf looked after Asghar and Afshan that just last month they had given him money to study further. And Abba had said that he would give Yusuf a job at the factory once his studies were done. And now the same Yusuf was plotting to murder them.

Afshan was so scared that she found herself shivering. Tears poured down her cheeks. But she didn't dare cry loudly in case her brother heard her. She didn't want him to be upset any more. She guessed how worried he must be about what would happen to Abba and Ammi. She felt she was in the throes of a nightmare. If only she could wake up and find it was actually one.

Ashok heard the clock strike 11. Another hour and Vishnu and the others would be here. He began struggling to get his hands free. But Yusuf had tied them really tightly.

Just then he heard a sound at the window. He lay still and listened. Who was it?

By now his eyes had got used to the darkness and he could see quite well. He saw a small head rise cautiously over the windowsill and peep in. But he could not make out who it was.

"Bhaiya? Bhaijaan? Are you there?" the person called out in a soft whisper.

Ashok almost cried in relief. He had recognized Chotu's voice.

"Bhaiya? Ashok Bhaiya?" Chotu called again.

But none of the children could answer. What could he do, Ashok wondered. Then he had an idea. He thumped with his feet at the bedpost.

Chotu heard the sound and whispered again: "Is that you Ashok Bhaiya?"

Ashok thumped again. Chotu jimmied the window with a wire and climbed in. He stood there for a second, trying to peer into the darkness. Then he made out a dark shape near the bed. He went closer and touched him.

"Ashok Bhaiya?" he asked, in a soft voice. Ashok wriggled in answer.

Now Chotu could see much more clearly. He realized that Ashok was tied up. He tried to open the knots, but couldn't do so in the dark. He dared not put on the light. Then he saw that Ashok's mouth seemed to be gagged. He reached out and pulled it down.

Ashok breathed in relief.

"Thank you, Chotu. Now listen, I want you to do something. The attack on the Khans is planned for tonight, not tomorrow," he said.

"I know, Ashok Bhaiya. Priya realised that when she saw that there was no moon. She wanted to tell your parents, but they had gone out. That is why I decided to come and see whether I could help you."

"Okay, now I want you to go as fast as you can get help from either Papa or Srivastava Chacha. You know where he lives, right?" Ashok asked.

"Yes, I do. It is quite far, but don't worry. I will run as fast as I can," Chotu said.

"Okay then, now hurry. There is no time to be lost," said Ashok.

Chotu ran to the window and jumped out.

Ashok felt slightly better. Now if only Chotu could find someone in time.

Now that his gag was off he could at least talk.

He called out to Asghar. He hard a soft thump on the

floor in reply. Another thump told him that Afshan was also listening to him.

"Listen, you two. Don't worry. I am sure Chotu will find someone. And they will call the police and come here soon. Nothing will happen to either of you or your parents, I am sure," Ashok said.

He felt he had to somehow give his friends hope. He wished Chotu would hurry up and get help. What was the time? There was no way of telling in the dark.

He felt his legs getting cramped. He rolled on the floor trying to find a more comfortable position. In the process he pulled at the bedcover and something fell on to the floor with a loud clatter.

What was that? He froze. Had anyone heard that? But no one came in to investigate. He crept up to the object and felt it with his feet. What was it? Then he knew.

Of course, it was the knife that Yusuf had brought with him. He had left it on the bed when he was tying up the children. And then he had forgotten to pick it up when he left.

Suddenly Ashok had an idea. He turned himself till his tied-up wrists were close to the knife. Then holding it between two fingers, he tried to rub it against the rope. It was awkward but Ashok set his teeth and kept on rubbing.

Would his idea work?

## CHAPTER 9
# CHOTU TO THE RESCUE

As soon as Chotu had leapt down from the window, he ran as fast as he could. He was careful to stay in the shadows. He ran down the road till he came to the same neem tree.

Now where should he go for help? It was no use going home as Ma and Babuji were out.

He had two choices. He could either run to Srivastava Chacha's house which was a good twenty minutes away or he could go to the police station, which was much closer.

But then Ashok Bhaiya had asked him to go to Srivastava Chacha's house. Maybe he had better go there.

He set off at a run. Soon the little boy was panting. But he couldn't afford to stop. There was no time to lose. He came to the park. He could cut across it and reach Srivastava Chacha's house much faster. The only thing was, the park was open and he could be seen quite easily. He decided to take the risk and set off across the park.

Suddenly he heard a whistle. He turned around. He could see someone running after him. Who was it? But there was no time to stop and find out.

Chotu ran faster. He managed to reach the other gate of the park. By now the man was gaining on him. Chotu felt his lungs would burst. He had to rest. But if he stopped, he would be caught. Then he saw a pipal tree outside the park gates. He quickly clung to a low branch and pulled himself up. He lay on a wide branch and tried to get back his breath. He was panting so loudly that he was sure he could be heard quite far away.

For a while, all that Chotu could hear was his own breathing and his heart thudding. Once he had regained his breath, he strained to listen for the footsteps of his pursuer.

At first he could hear nothing. Then he heard someone coming towards the park gates. The person stood at the gates and looked here and there. Chotu peered through the leaves and held his breath. Would the man realise that the person he had been chasing was hidden up in the tree?

Who was the man? Chotu couldn't see his face. If it had been a moonlit night he would have had no problem.

The man came and stood under tree. Just then another man came from the other lane and joined the first man. For the second time that night Chotu found himself peering down from a tree on a meeting.

"How is it going?" the second man asked.

"It was all fine till just now. As I was walking down Hilton Road I saw someone running across the park. I called out to him to stop, but he only ran faster. I chased him, but lost him around here," the first man said.

"Who was it? Did you manage to make out?" asked the second man.

"No, Srivastava, I didn't. But the funny thing is that I think the person was only a child. Who would let a child roam around at this time of the night in these times?" asked the first man.

Chotu's heart leapt with pleasure. Srivastava? What luck! He had been trying to get to Srivastava Chacha's house and here he was just near him. He quickly slithered down the tree and stood near the two men.

"Hey! Who are you?" asked the man who had been called Srivastava.

"Babuji, I am Chotu. I work at Guptaji's house."

"Chotu, what are you doing here? Is anything wrong?"

Mr Srivastava asked.

"I was coming to your house, Babuji. Ashok Bhaiya sent me," Chotu said.

"Then why did you run when I chased you?" the other man asked.

"Doesn't matter, Bhawani Shankar. Let us hear what the boy has to say," said Mr Srivastava.

"Babuji, Ashok Bhaiya is in great danger. He is at the Khans' house. And some men are planning to attack the Khans at midnight tonight. Please do something, Babuji," Chotu begged, tugging at Mr Srivastava's kurta in his anxiety.

"Don't worry, Chotu. You go home and stay there. We will take care of this. Come, Bhawani Shankar, there is not a moment to lose. You go to the police station and inform them while I rush to Khan's house. Hurry up!" And both men set off at a run.

Chotu turned to set off home. But then he felt he couldn't just go home and sit there waiting for news. He decided he would return to Asghar's house and return home with Ashok Bhaiya.

So instead of making tracks for the Guptas' house, Chotu set off in a roundabout way to reach Asghar's house. He did not want to go across the park again. He hadn't forgotten his run earlier.

Meanwhile what was happening at the Khans'?

We had left Ashok trying to cut through his bonds with a knife. But it was an awkward business as his wrists were tied together. He couldn't hurry either as he might end up cutting himself. But the same determination that had led him to work for hours together trying to set up the "telephone" system between his house and his friend's kept him going now too. At last, after what seemed like hours to him, he felt the bonds give a little. He wrenched his hand apart and found his hands free.

For a while he sat there rubbing his wrists trying to get the blood circulation going in his hands once again. Yusuf, or Ramu to give him his right name, had tied his hands so tight that they had become numb.

Once his hands felt normal once again, he crawled to Asghar and untied his gag.

"Asghar, don't talk too loud in case anyone hears. I am going to untie your hands and then we will release Afshan," Ashok whispered.

"Fine," Asghar whispered back. "But what are we going to about Yusuf?"

"I don't know, but once we are free we can try to at least stop the men," said Ashok as he untied Asghar's wrists.

Then he released Afshan from her bonds while Asghar tried to get the circulation back in his fingers.

"Listen, Asghar, you and I will go and see whether it is

safe outside. If it is then we will go to your father and tell him everything," Ashok whispered.

"Okay, but Afshan had better stay here. She is still weak and won't be able to run as fast as we can if need be," said Asghar.

"Yeah, that is a good idea," Ashok agreed. Afshan was relieved. She didn't feel she had enough energy to even walk to the door, let alone run.

Just then they heard someone at the door. Ashok was desperate. Suppose it was Yusuf come to check on them? He shouldn't know that they had managed to untie themselves.

"Quick hold your hands behind you and bend down," he told Asghar and Afshan. They did as he said. Afshan even shook her hair over her face so that a casual glance would not reveal that her gag was off.

It was a good idea. For, it was Yusuf come to check on the children. Luckily he didn't switch on the lights. He merely flashed a torch in and once he saw the children crouched on the floor he went out, locking the door behind him.

Once his footsteps faded away, Ashok asked Asghar, "How do we go out of the room? He has locked it behind him."

"Don't worry," said Asghar. "Afshan and I discovered only recently that my cupboard key can unlock my room as well. One day Afshan locked me in for a joke and I tried the key and found it opened the door quite easily."

He went to the cupboard and took out the key. He carefully put it in the keyhole. It was a tight fit but after a bit of jiggling it gave a reassuring click. Asghar opened the door and peeped into the corridor.

It was dark and quiet. Everyone had gone to bed. He heard the ticking of the grandfather clock in the corridor, but didn't know what the time was exactly. It was late enough if even his father had gone to bed. He crept down the corridor, Ashok close behind him. They came to a stop outside Asghar's parents' room.

Asghar quietly opened the door and the two boys slipped in.

"Ammi? Abba?" Asghar called in a whisper. There was no answer. His parents must be fast asleep, Asghar decided. He went closer to the bed and put out his hand to shake them awake.

But what was this? His hand met just the sheet. He felt around. There was no one in the bed. He reached out to the table beside the bed and felt around for the torch that he knew was always kept there. He found it and flashed it for a second. That was enough to show him that his parents' bed was empty.

Ashok let out a soft exclamation. Where were Asif Chacha and Nafisa Chachi?

"Let us go and check the study," Asghar whispered. The two went out of the room and silently walked down the corridor to the main wing where the study was.

Just as they reached the end of the corridor, which opened into a large hallway from where various rooms opened off, they heard a loud cry.

"What is the matter?" they heard Asif Chacha ask. "Who are these people, Yusuf?"

Ashok realised the attackers had already entered the house.

"Not Yusuf, Khan Sahab, but Ramu. I am Ramu. Vishnu sent me here for just this night," they heard Yusuf say.

"Yes, Khan Sahab, that day when you sent me away in disgrace, you didn't think that one day you would be standing in front of me, did you? Now let us see whether you win or I do," they heard a man say, venom dripping from his words.

"Oh no, you won't do anything to my father," shouted Asghar as he ran to the study. Ashok had no choice, but to run with his friend. There was no way he was going to let him face those villains alone.

"The men turned around for a second. That was enough for Mr Khan to rush forward and tackle one of the men. While he fought one of them, the boys attacked the others. But they were five and more than enough match for

Mr Khan and the two boys. Yusuf held Asghar in a vice-like grip while another man did the same to Ashok. Two others held Mr Khan while Vishnu took out an ugly looking knife.

"This is the end for you, Khan. I told you that day at the factory that I would pay you back. Now it is my turn," he said.

But as he lifted his hand to strike Mr Khan, he gave a loud yelp. The next moment the knife went flying from hand and he bent double in pain. Ashok looked at the window and saw Chotu perched there. A large stone lay near Vishnu.

Taking advantage of their captors' attention being diverted Asghar and Ashok twisted out of their grip. They began pummeling the men as hard as they could. But they didn't have to go on long as there was loud banging on the door. The men looked at one another in consternation. But before they could do anything, they heard footsteps running to the main door. In a trice it was opened and the police poured into the house.

Ashok took in a deep breath. He had saved his friend's family. He felt spent. He could not be even bother to wonder how the police had reached there. All that could wait till later.

**CHAPTER 10**
# THREE CHEERS FOR FREEDOM

It was the next day that Ashok and Priya, Asghar and Afshan learnt the whole story. The night before, once everything was over, the villains arrested and taken away, the children had fallen into such deep sleep that they woke up only the next day at noon. No one woke them up till the bright sunlight crept into their rooms and on to their beds.

Once they were awake, Ashok and Priya were impatient to know all about the events of the night before. So they quickly dressed and ran downstairs. They found Asghar and Afshan sitting at the dining table chatting with Ma and Papa.

"When did you two come?" Ashok and Priya exclaimed together as they ran to welcome their friends.

"Just now. Ammi and Abba are also here," said Afshan, looking pale still but much better.

Just then Asif Chacha and Papa walked in.

"Hello, children! Ashok, I must congratulate you on your bravery last night. You proved yourself a true friend," Mr Khan said.

Ashok went red with pleasure.

"But it would have been much more sensible to have told me what you were about to do," said Papa. "Then you needn't have run unnecessary risks."

"Papa, I did try to. But you were not here," Ashok said.

"Not an excuse really. You should have tried harder. If you had told me as soon as you heard the conversation outside the window, I would have informed the patrolling committee and we would have been at the Khans' place much earlier," explained Papa. "But you must be congratulated on your loyalty to your friend."

"Papa, tell us what happened last night. The whole story," Priya begged. "I wasn't there and know very little."

"Well, you can hear everything over lunch," said Ma, walking in with Nafisa Chachi. "Asha is just bringing in the food."

"Good! I am so hungry I could eat an elephant," Ashok said.

While they waited for Asha to serve lunch, Papa began telling the whole story.

"Actually, we had some inkling about what Vishnu and his friends were planning. We knew they were going to create trouble, but not what they were going to do. So we had already formed patrolling committees and last night everyone was out, keeping a lookout for trouble.

"But everything seemed normal. We had planned that if nothing happened by midnight, then we would go back home leaving just one person to continue with the patrolling as we do normally.

"It was just as we were about to call off the patrolling that Chotu met Srivastava and Bhawani Shankar. As soon as they learnt that the attack was on the Khans' house, Srivastava went to inform the rest of the patrol members while Bhawani Shankar went to the police station.

"The police had already been warned to be ready by Chatterjee and they were able to reach the Khans' house within minutes.

"We thought we would have to break down the door, but to our surprise it was opened for us."

"Who opened the door, Papa?" Ashok asked.

"I don't know. I was behind the police so I didn't see.

I thought one of you boys did it," said Mr Gupta.

"Actually I did it," said Nafisa Chachi. The others looked at her in surprise.

"How did you know it was the police?" Asif Chacha asked.

"I couldn't sleep and then I realised that I had not heated the jeera pani for Afshan for the morning. Her throat is still not completely alright and I wanted her to drink it in the morning. So I went to the kitchen to see if the cook had heated it. While I was there I heard the commotion in the study. I was wondering what to do when I heard the jeeps. I peeped out of the window and saw the police. So I ran to the door and opened it as they began knocking on it," she explained.

"Bravo, Ammi. If it hadn't been for you the men might have hurt us before the police got in. Or they might have run away," said Asghar.

"But the real hero in all this is Chotu," said Priya, smiling at the small boy as he walked in behind Asha, carrying the plates.

"Yes. If he hadn't told us we would not have realised that Vishnu planned to attack last night. And he was the one who saved Asif Chacha by throwing the stone at Vishnu," said Ashok.

"That is right. Chotu, you deserve a reward. What do

you want?" asked Asif Chacha.

"Can I really ask for anything?" asked Chotu in wonder.

"Yes, you can. What do you want?" asked Asif Uncle again.

"I want a bottle of the lotion that Priya applied on me when Kumar beat me up," said Chotu.

"But why Chotu? No one will beat you ever again," Papa said gently.

"Really, Babuji? Never?" asked Chotu in wonder.

"Never," assured Papa. "Now what else do you want?"

"Then Babuji, I just want to live with Ashok and Priya forever. They are my best friends," he said.

"And you are ours," Ashok and Priya said together.

"And ours too," Asghar and Afshan chorused.

"Well, Chotu, you will always live with us. And once things are back to normal you will study just like Ashok and Priya and get educated," said Papa. Chotu was so happy that he could only smile.

Just then Asha walked in with the lunch. She had made aloo paranthas.

"Yummy! This adventure began with aloo paranthas and is ending with it as well," said Ashok.

"Yes, three cheers for aloo paranthas," said Asghar.

"Three cheers for friends," said Asif Chacha, smiling around the table. And the room resounded with cheers.

# EPILOGUE

"And that is the story of our adventure," said Priya Nani.

Praveen, Prashant, Amisha and Payal had been listening spellbound.

"And what an adventure, Priya Nani. I wish we could have an adventure," said Praveen with a sigh.

"Yes, you seemed to have lived through such interesting times," said Amisha.

"They were hard times. I still can't forget the fear I lived through that night, waiting for Ashok Bhaiya to return. Till he did I didn't know whether he would return alive or not," said Priya Nani, giving an involuntary shiver.

"No wonder you and Ashok Nana and Asghar Uncle and Afshan Aunty have remained such good friends," said Payal.

"Yes, there is nothing like shared trouble to strengthen friendships. But now you know why Ashok Nana says that he would never spend Independence Day anywhere but in Delhi. He realised how important independence and freedom was that night when he thought he would lose all that he held most dear.

And now it is up to you children to see that the freedom that India won with so much difficulty stays intact," said Priya Nani.

The children felt the truth of her remarks much more than when the Principal had said something similar at the school assembly that morning. After listening to Priya Nani's tale, Praveen and Prashant felt they should do everything possible to save India's freedom.

And I am sure they will always remember that, even after they grow up. Or, as Prashant said, every time they eat aloo paranthas!